This book must be returned by the date specified at the time of issue as the DUE DATE FOR RETURN

The loan may be extended (personally, by post, telephone or online) for a further period, if the book is not required by another reader, by quoting the barcode / author / title.

Enquiries: 01709 336774

www.rotherham.gov.uk/libraries

BR

The Pirates and the Talent Show

By Adam and Charlotte Guillain

Illustrated by Rupert Van Wyk

W
FRANKLIN WATTS
LONDON•SYDNEY

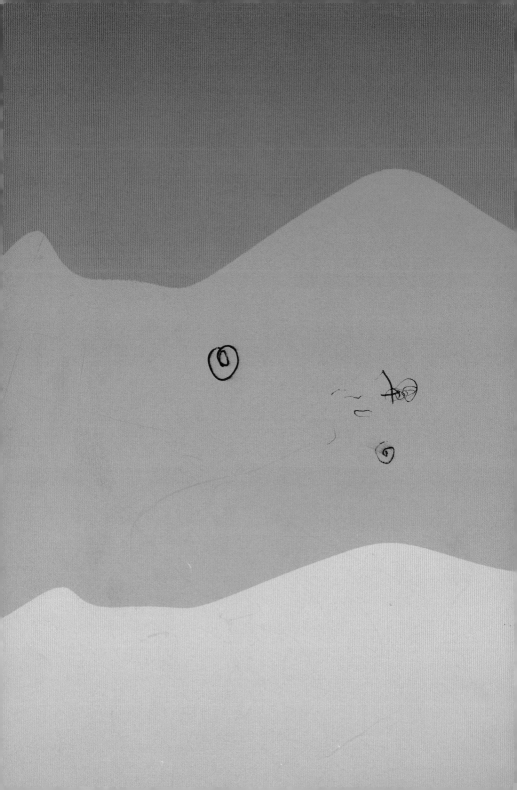

Chapter 1

The Planktown Pirates loved scaring

sailors. They loved digging for treasure.

But they did not love cleaning.

"I'm tired of mopping the deck," groaned

Manta Ray Jack, the ship's first mate.

"Cleaning is boring," said Cook Cockles.

"But the ship is a tip," sighed Captain Cuttlefish. "Let's have a good old sing and dance while we get the job done!" It wasn't long before every living thing for miles knew it was cleaning day on board the pirate ship.

"I love singing," sang Manta Ray Jack
as he washed the sails.

"Singing and dancing is what we do best,"
trilled Cook Cockles as he washed the pots
and pans.

"We should be in a band!" declared
Captain Cuttlefish as he danced around
the deck with a broom.

The Planktown Pirates loved singing and
dancing. The trouble was, they were
rubbish. The cats yowled. The dogs howled.

"Please be quiet," said Connor the Cabin
Boy, sticking his fingers into his ears.
But no one heard him. They were all too
busy making a horrible din.

After a while, Cook Cockles said,

"I'm running out of soap."

"Me too," said Manta Ray Jack.

"Time to go to the shops," declared

Captain Cuttlefish.

Chapter 2

The Planktown Pirates went ashore and
filled their bags with soap. As they walked
back to the ship, Cook Cockles suddenly
stopped. "Hey Captain, look at this,"
he said, pointing to a poster.

"A talent show!" cried Manta Ray Jack.

"We should enter it!" roared Captain Cuttlefish.

"And do what?" asked Connor.

"We can sing!" said Manta Ray Jack.

"And dance!" said Cook Cockles.

"You can't sing or dance," said Connor, pleadingly. "Can't you do something else?" But no one heard him. They were too excited, planning what they were all going to do in the talent show.

In fact, the Planktown Pirates were so excited, they didn't even care when it started to rain. Even worse, they didn't notice their arch-rivals, the Gruesome Crew, peering round the corner.

"So they're planning to enter the talent show, eh?" muttered Captain Sharkfin, with an evil laugh. "They haven't got a chance."

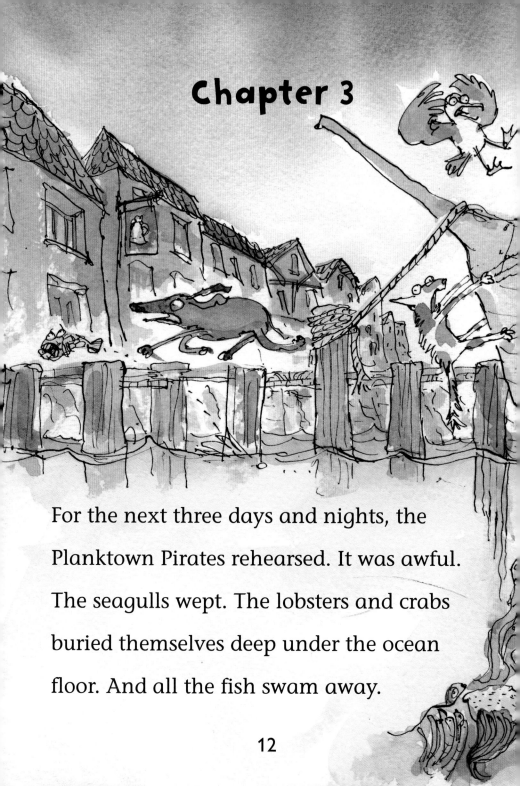

Chapter 3

For the next three days and nights, the
Planktown Pirates rehearsed. It was awful.
The seagulls wept. The lobsters and crabs
buried themselves deep under the ocean
floor. And all the fish swam away.

Connor had to get off the ship. He rowed all the way to the other side of the island. "Oh no!" he gulped when he spotted a ship. "It's the Gruesome Crew!"

Connor rowed a little closer to see what he could discover. He could hear the Gruesome Crew singing a sea shanty and stamping their feet on the deck of their ship.

"They're good!" he gasped. "If they enter the talent show, the Planktown Pirates haven't got a chance!"

Chapter 4

It was the night of the talent show and the

Planktown Pirates were very excited.

"We're the last to perform," said Captain

Cuttlefish, peering at his programme.

Connor was relieved that there was no mention of the Gruesome Crew anywhere. "Maybe they're not coming after all," he thought, hopefully.

Then the talent show began. First, there was a juggling sailor.

Next up, there was a salty sea dog and his cartwheeling puppy.

Then came a team of windsurfing women
playing wind instruments.

"They're all rather good!" said Captain
Cuttlefish, nervously.

"And now for a very special treat," said the announcer. "Please put your hands together for the best pirate singers to sail the seven seas."

"That must be us," said Captain Cuttlefish, getting to his feet.

"A late addition to our programme –
the Gruesome Crew!" cheered the
announcer.

"Our arch-enemies!" cried Captain
Cuttlefish. "What are they doing here?"

"Maybe they'll be rubbish," quivered
Manta Ray Jack.

But the Gruesome Crew were not rubbish. They sang in harmony and stomped and shuffled their boots in perfect rhythm. When they were done, the Gruesome Crew got a huge cheer. "Quick, we've got to get out of here!" said Captain Cuttlefish, hurrying his men away.

Chapter 5

The Planktown Pirates were just tip-toeing away when Captain Sharkfin grabbed the microphone. "Put your hands together for the Planktown Pirates – the worst singers and dancers to sail the seven seas!"

The cats yowled. The dogs howled. But the talent show crowd cheered as Captain Cuttlefish and his men were bundled onto the stage. "I feel sick," said Manta Ray Jack.

"This is going to be fun," sniggered Captain Sharkfin. As the Planktown Pirates began to sing and dance, the Gruesome Crew did gruesome things. They slipped lobsters into the Planktown Pirates' boots. They put jellyfish in their hats.

But as the lobsters snapped and the jellyfish stung, something amazing happened. The Planktown Pirates leapt and shrieked in pain. "Wow!" gasped the crowd. "Their voices are so high. And look how they can jump!"

The Planktown Pirates danced and sang like never before. They finished by forming a stunning pirate pyramid and hitting the highest note ever sung by a pirate crew. It was incredible.

"I knew we could win," said Captain
Cuttlefish as the Planktown Pirates limped
back to the ship.

"I just wasn't expecting it to be so painful,"
groaned Manta Ray Jack.

"Maybe next time we enter a talent show we should try something different," suggested Cook Cockles.

"Like what?" said Captain Cuttlefish.

"Like listening to me," said Connor the Cabin Boy, with a grin.

Franklin Watts
First published in Great Britain in 2015 by
The Watts Publishing Group

Text © Adam and Charlotte Guillain 2015
Illustrations © Rupert Van Wyk 2015

Series Editor: Melanie Palmer
Series Advisor: Catherine Glavina
Cover Design: Cathryn Gilbert
Design Manager: Peter Scoulding

ISBN 978 1 4451 4123 7 (hbk)
ISBN 978 1 4451 4124 4 (pbk)
ISBN 978 1 4451 4126 8 (library ebook)

Printed in China

Franklin Watts
An imprint of
Hachette Children's Group
Part of The Watts Publishing Group
Carmelite House
50 Victoria Embankment
London EC4Y 0DZ

An Hachette UK Company
www.hachette.co.uk

www.franklinwatts.co.uk